Over the Hills to NUGGET

By Aileen Fisher

Cover Design by Elle Staples

Cover illustration by Tatiana Glebova

This unabridged version has updated grammar and spelling.

First published in 1949

© 2018 Jenny Phillips

Table of Contents

1. You Never Can Tell 1
2. What's the Hurry, Son? 4
3. Six Surprises 7
4. Part of Another Life 12
5. Pay Your Toll 16
6. Nugget Camp 21
7. The Surprises Come True 26
8. Cornmeal and Dried Apples 33
9. The House with the Tower 38
10. Ernie's Treat 43
11. A Ride on Lake Michigan 47
12. Heap Red Strawberry Jam 51
13. A Morning Caller 54
14. The Deal's Off 63
15. A Strange New Voice 66
16. Long After Bedtime 69
17. A Surprise Trip to Town 73
18. Smoke on the Wind 77
19. The Grass Will Grow Again 82

You Never Can Tell

For the sixth day in a row, Ernie stood waiting for the stagecoach to come with the mail. For the sixth day he listened to the mine whistles blowing the noon hour. He had an empty feeling inside of him. What had happened to Papa? Had he found a job in another gold mine? Why hadn't he written? Didn't he know how hard it was to stay behind, waiting and waiting for a letter?

Ernie counted the boards in the sidewalk in front of the General Store and Post Office. The number was just the same as yesterday, and the day before.

A freight wagon pulled by two mules and four horses creaked up the road, sending a cloud of dust into the dry May air. Behind the wagon came an old man leading a burro with a big pack on its back. Then another wagon, pulled by four oxen, but no stage! No mail!

Slim Perkins, from the livery stable next door, came over. He was always on hand to tend to the stage horses. "Still waiting for that letter, Ernie?" he asked.

"Yes, sir."

"Stage ought to be along any minute now." Slim pulled out a big gold watch, with a nugget on the watch chain. "Can't expect it to break a record every day." He studied the watch, then slipped it back in his pocket.

"Guess your Pa wasn't so far wrong about going to hunt for another job. Heard the Crown o' Gold laid off twenty men this morning."

"Honest? My father said the ore was pinching out."

"Don't know what will happen to Skillet Gulch if the Crown o' Gold shuts down, now that the Yankee Doodle and the Glory are slowing up."

"Maybe someone will make another strike."

"Maybe." Slim pushed back his wide-brimmed hat and leaned against the hitching post. "You never can tell. You never can tell about anything, least of all gold mines."

Ernie looked across at the steep hillside spotted with mines and holes and ore dumps. From the lower part of the gulch came the bang, bang, pound, pound of the stamp mills. Ernie often watched the big iron weights go up and down, stamping the ore to dust so the gold could be washed out.

"There's the stage now!" Slim shouted.

Around the turn where the road climbed up the gulch

came a swaying coach. The four horses were going a good clip for a mountain road, and the harness bells jangled loudly. It was the stage, all right.

Slim pulled out his watch again. "Well, I'll be . . ." he grunted. "Ott made it a good two minutes earlier than yesterday. That's shaving it pretty close."

The dust-covered Concord coach jolted to a stop at the stepping stone in front of the store. Ernie always admired the red, white, and blue harness rings, and the plumes on the horses. He liked the harness bells that warned other teams to turn out. It must be wonderful to drive a stage!

Slim hurried to unhitch the tired horses and hitch up fresh ones. Ott Jones, the driver, jumped down from his high seat up front and stretched before opening the door for the six shaken, dusty passengers. Then he threw off the mail sacks.

Ernie's heart beat hard, as if he had been running. Would there be a letter from Papa? He remembered what Slim had said just a few minutes before. "You never can tell." That was the way about the mail. You never could tell, looking at the outside of a mail bag, what there was inside.

What's the Hurry, Son?

Up the hilly street Ernie raced, with something white in his hand. Past the Home Sweet Home Hotel that always smelled of beer and onions. Past the Miners' Pride saloon, the newspaper office, the blacksmith shop. Past Gus Kline's butcher shop, and Ed's Place. At the end of the board walk, he almost bumped into a pair of buckskin trousers.

"What's the hurry, son?"

"We got a letter!" Ernie shouted, as he raced along. It seemed everyone must know how it felt to get a letter.

Mama would be so glad! Especially, Ernie thought, if Papa had found a better job and a better house to live in. Becca would tell everyone. Florie would listen with big eyes and never say a word.

Wasn't Florie ever going to talk, Ernie wondered? Papa said Becca talked so much that Florie didn't need to. Mama said maybe it was because Florie fell out of the covered wagon when she was a tiny baby and hurt her tongue. That was almost four years ago, in 1868, when they were coming across the plains to Colorado Territory.

"There comes Ernie. There comes Ernie," Becca sang out from her post on the rickety stoop of the cabin. "And he's got a letter, Mama!"

Mama appeared at the door with little Bibby in her arms. Florie, perching on the stoop, looked like a strange little bird with big eyes.

Ernie climbed the path to the patch of level ground held by the wall of stones Papa had fixed in front of the cabin. Most of the houses in Skillet Gulch hung on the hillsides, in uneven rows. It sometimes seemed that a big wind might send them all sliding downhill.

Panting, Ernie handed the letter to Mama. "It came," he said. Then he flopped down on the stoop, wishing his heart would stop pounding so hard in his ears, but he knew that was what came of running uphill when you lived a mile and a half above sea level!

Mama was eager. She took the letter quickly and turned it over. Ernie wondered if she would tear it open right away or wait to get a knife—the way she usually did.

Even when she was in a hurry, Mama wanted things to be neat. That was why mining camps like Skillet Gulch bothered her so much. The houses were sprawly and dirty, and the hills around were spoiled by all the mining and digging. Mama had not wanted to come west in the first place. She wanted to stay in Michigan, on the farm next to Grandpa's, but Papa . . .

"It's postmarked from Nugget," Mama said. "That's thirty or thirty-five miles over the hills."

Ernie looked up. Eagerly she was tearing open the letter. For once she didn't wait to get a knife!

Six Surprises

"Nugget, Colorado Territory, 24 May, 1872," Mama read out loud.

Dear Wife Sarah:

Forgive me for not writing sooner. Until today I had no good news for you. Now I have many surprises—a big one for all of you, and a little one for each.

"Just like Papa," Mama said, looking up from the page. Ernie saw that her eyes were glad for the first time in days. She turned back to the letter:

For you, Sarah, my wife, I have the surprise of a sound. It will make you think that Michigan is right under your feet again. For you, Ernie, my son, I have the surprise of something round and cool, smaller than most, but quite big enough.

"What can it be?" Ernie asked. "Something round and cool . . ."

"Well," said Becca, who always had an answer for everything, "it could be a watermelon."

Ernie made a face, and Mama started to read again:

For Rebecca, my eldest daughter, I have the surprise of a little brown cup, with four inside, and one on top.

"Four what?" wondered Becca.

For my quiet daughter, Florie, who is going to talk one of these days, I have something soft and warm and the color of a thundercloud.

Florie listened, blinked, but said not a word.

For my baby daughter, Elizabeth, better known as Bibby, I have something tall and stately, and its name is Queen Elizabeth. Think of that.

"Five surprises," Ernie said, "and we don't know what a single one of them really is."

"If we did know," Becca put in, "they wouldn't be surprises."

Now for the big surprise! I have bought a mountain ranch! It has a two-room cabin, and a shed, and a wonderful spring of water. It is just about three miles from Nugget camp.

"A ranch!" Ernie knew by the tone of Mama's voice that she was glad. "Now we won't have to live in a mining camp anymore," she said. "But I wonder where the money came from, to buy a ranch."

The letter explained everything.

> *Of course, I didn't have enough money to pay Charley Whiskers the full price for his ranch, but he is in no hurry. He wants to go looking for gold again, and the ranch ties him down. You know how prospectors are!*
>
> *I got a good buy on the place, and I am full of plans for it. We can cut and sell the wild hay in the meadow. There is plenty of game around, and a trout stream a mile away. We must get some cows. With prices what they are in the mining camps, we can do well selling butter and milk. The land looks good for growing potatoes. If things come to the worst, I can always get a job in Nugget at one of the mines or stamp mills.*

Papa had thought it all out. He said Mama was right about mining. Only a few lucky people ever struck it rich. The others broke their backs panning gold in the creeks or pounding their lives away in tunnels. If they got a couple of dollars a day for their work, they were lucky.

Yes, Mama was right. The mines were dark and wet, and the air smelled of burned powder. Dirt and rocks slid down; dripping water rotted the timbers that held the walls. It was no life for a man who was raised on a farm and liked the sun!

Papa went on:

> *I am glad we kept the wagon and the horses. Ernie will have to take Old Nell and Jim to the blacksmith's for new shoes. Then pack our belongings on the wagon, and drive to Nugget as soon as you can. I will be at Parsons' General Store in Nugget on the afternoon of the 28th. You should be there by then, if all goes well. You know what I always say—"The best is always ahead!" Well, it surely is this time, over the hills to Nugget.*

"Oh, I hope so," Mama said, sort of under her breath.

The letter was signed:

> *Your loving husband and father, Willis Brett.*

Then there was a postscript:

> *Dear Ernie, I am counting on you to take good care of the women folks.*

Mama and Ernie and Becca all started to talk at once about the new ranch, and packing up, and Papa's plans. There were so many things to think about. Silent little

Florie got up from the stoop and slipped into the house. Becca looked after her.

"I wonder if Florie understands what was in the letter," Becca whispered.

Ernie, who was nearest the door, peeked in. Soon he said softly: "Florie is packing her old rag doll and doll clothes in a box. Maybe Florie can't talk, but she knows."

Part of Another Life

Becca told Susan Jenks, who lived in the shanty three doors away, and Susan told her mother:

"They're going to move to Nugget, Ma—to a ranch. They're going to start in the morning. Maybe they wouldn't want to take the caster along, Ma, over the rough roads. The little bottles might break. Maybe they'd sell it . . . if you asked them."

Mrs. Jenks looked up from her wash tub. "We've never had anything so fine as caster, and there's that money I saved from washing."

"It's real silver, the part with holes in where the bottles fit," continued Susan. "And it turns. So if the salt is in front of you when you want the pepper, you just turn it a little."

"Same with the oil bottle and vinegar, isn't it?"

"Yes, Ma, and the little bottles are carved all over with flowers and things."

Mrs. Jenks wiped her hands on her flour sack apron. "I reckon I'll go over and ask about that caster, Susan. Seems a family isn't really somebody 'less they have a caster."

There was so much to do Mama kept right on packing when Mrs. Jenks came and stood in the doorway. Ernie kept bringing in things from the kitchen.

"I'm not likin' to see you move, Miz Brett." Mrs. Jenks tucked up one corner of her apron to cover a dirty spot. She looked around at the clothes and blankets and pots and pans Mama was packing. The round-top trunk was almost full, and several boxes too, but the caster was still on the table. The silver of it shone in the sunlight, and the glass sparkled like diamonds.

Mrs. Jenks could hardly take her eyes off it. "If you think that caster would be hard to pack, Miz Brett, I'll make you an offer for it. I'll pay you ten dollars."

Mama gave a little start. Ten dollars! That was a lot of money.

"Yes, Miz Brett. Ten dollars."

Ernie looked at Mama, wondering what she would do. Ten dollars would buy part of a cow . . .

Mama stopped packing, and stared at the caster. Then she said slowly, "Thank you, Mrs. Jenks. That's a real good price. Ten dollars would mean a lot to us right now. But, you see . . . I don't know how to say it . . . that caster is part of another life to me. I got it for a wedding present, in Michigan. I just don't think I could bear to part with it."

Mrs. Jenks sighed. "I never had a caster, but I know what you mean. If you wrap each of the bottles up in paper, they ought to ride all right."

Ernie saw that Mrs. Jenks felt badly not to have the caster. She stood there in the doorway, big and heavy, and a little bent over. "Maybe Mrs. Jenks would like to see the Star of Bethlehem again, before we pack it," Ernie suggested.

Mrs. Jenks brightened up. "That patch quilt with the big star in the middle and all the little eight-point stars around the sides? I sure would like to see it again."

Mama lifted up a bundle carefully wrapped in pink outing flannel. "Mr. Brett says it's our most valuable belonging," she smiled, as she opened the bundle. "It took me two years, odd times, to make it, before I was married. I haven't used it once since we came to Colorado Territory."

"I should think not," sniffed Mrs. Jenks. "Not a beautiful quilt like that, in a miner's cabin." She leaned over to admire the hundreds and hundreds of little diamond-shaped patches in the stars, and all the tiny stitches.

Mama looked around the room. "Would you like the geraniums, Mrs. Jenks?" she asked suddenly, glad that there was something nice for her neighbor to have. "They will be hard for us to pack. Ernie can help you carry them home."

So Ernie helped Mrs. Jenks carry home the flower pots. On the way back he stood for a moment beside the cabin, on the dry hillside, with blue and gold sky around him. The air smelled good, and it seemed to have wings, it was so light.

For many months this little cabin had been home—and these rocky hills full of mines, and the gulch with its winding road and noisy mills and strings of shanties. "Part of another life," Mama had said about the caster. Would Skillet Gulch seem like part of another life when they were settled on the new ranch? Ernie wondered.

Pay Your Toll

By late afternoon the next day they had gone twelve or fifteen miles from Skillet Gulch. They were long, warm, jiggly miles. All day the sun burned down through a yellow hole in the sky. The hills and mountains marched on and on, some of them with white heads, some with their arms full of trees.

Ernie did most of the driving, sitting up in the wagon seat next to Mama, who held Bibby in her lap. Behind, in the wagon box, on top of the old canvas that covered the bedding and boxes and tubs and buckets, Becca and Florie made themselves a place to sit.

Ernie felt very proud that Mama let him drive so much. The roads were so narrow and winding. Sometimes he had to pull hard on the hand brake to keep the wagon from going too fast down a hill. Other times, when he heard the harness bells of freight wagons or saw a driver's dog come running ahead, he had to find a place to turn out and wait for the heavy wagons to pass.

Once when Ernie was driving along a shelf-like road curving through a canyon, Old Nell and Jim suddenly came face to face with a team of oxen pulling a covered wagon. There was no way to pass. Ernie had to back up a long way. Florie held on to Becca's dress, and Becca put her hands over her eyes.

"Take it easy, Ernie," Mama said quietly. "Old Nell will know how to do it. Don't get excited."

Mama was right. Old Nell was a smart horse. Papa always said: "Horses are like people. Some are smart, and some are just plain ordinary. Old Nell, now, belongs at the head of her class."

It was nice to have a horse you could depend on, Ernie thought, as he backed the wagon down the narrow road to a turn-out. Old Nell never got excited, and she always seemed to know what to do.

"We haven't made very good time," Mama said when they started ahead again, "but we got a late start. If we find a good camping place soon, perhaps we should stop. By pulling out early in the morning, we ought to reach Nugget by late afternoon."

"Just a little farther," Ernie urged. He was always eager to see what was beyond the next curve, and the sun was still two hours about setting.

"If we had four fast horses and a stagecoach, we'd get

there in a hurry," said Ernie, but then he knew a coach would be far too small for all their belongings.

The horses' new shoes clicked against the rocks in the road. What were all those surprises of Papa's? Ernie wondered. Something round and cool and smaller than most . . .

He looked sideways at Mama. Bibby was asleep, and Mama was gazing off across the mountains patched with great blue shadows. Was she wondering about the surprises too? About the sound that would make her think Michigan was right under her feet again?

Suddenly Ernie saw a sign: "Toll Gate Ahead."

Mama saw it too. "I thought there would be at least one toll gate between Skillet Gulch and Nugget. I wonder how much it costs to go through."

They drove up to the gate where a house sat almost on the road. There was another sign:

> **STOP**
>
> **WAGON AND TEAM - $1**
>
> **EACH EXTRA ANIMAL - $.25**

"A dollar for a wagon and team," Ernie repeated. "It costs a lot, doesn't it?"

"Yes." Mama reached in her dress pocket for the little buckskin coin purse that really belonged to Papa. "They have to pay for building the road and keeping it up, you see, besides wanting to make some money. I only hope there won't be another toll house before we get to Nugget."

"Whoa!" Ernie called, pulling back on the lines. The wagon came to a stop, and Mama took a silver dollar out of the purse.

"Pay your toll. Pay your toll," called a shrill voice.

Ernie looked around, but saw no one. Becca leaned over the wagon seat, between Ernie and Mama, and looked too.

"Pay your toll!" cried the shrill voice once more.

Just at that moment a tall woman, with a blue and white striped apron and sunbonnet to match, hurried out of the toll house. "That will be one dollar," she said. "You going far?"

Mama handed her the dollar. "We're going to Nugget. Do you know if there is another toll gate before we get there?"

"No, not going this-a-way. There are two if you go by Centerville."

"Pay your toll! Pay your toll!" came the shrill voice again.

Ernie gave a little jump and looked around. Mama frowned, turning her head quickly to one side, then to the other. Becca almost cried. "But we did pay," she burst out. "We did pay. We paid a whole silver dollar, didn't we, Mama?"

"Pay your toll."

The tall woman laughed, showing two spaces in the front of her mouth where there were no teeth. Then she pointed to a little pine tree beside the house. On one of the branches perched a black and white magpie, his long black tail gleaming almost blue in the sun.

"Pay your toll. Pay your toll," the magpie screeched.

Everyone laughed. Becca most of all.

"My son, Johnny, trained that magpie," the woman explained. "He split its tongue and trained it to talk. Now the sassy thing wants to show off all the time."

"Pay your toll. Pay your toll!" the pretty bird cried once more.

Nugget Camp

"We should soon be at Nugget camp," Mama said the next afternoon, as they passed the Nugget Stamp Mill. It was a wide slanting building, running down the hillside. Bang, bang, pound, pound went the weights that crushed the ore. Mama had to shout to be heard above the noise. "Perhaps near the top of the hill . . ."

Old Nell and Jim pulled the wagon up the long, rocky hill, and there lay Nugget camp, on a "saddle" between two small mountains.

"What a nice little place!" Mama exclaimed.

Ernie had never heard Mama call a mining camp nice before, but it did look better than other mining towns! The houses seemed to be better built—there was even paint on a few of them--and they were not so crowded together.

"I'm glad it isn't squeezed into a canyon," Mama said. She always felt that canyon walls pressed in on her and took her breath away, and she liked to see more sky than the narrow slit that showed above Skillet Gulch.

"What a nice place for a town," Mama repeated, as they passed the first log houses. "Look, Ernie, there's a real view in two directions. We couldn't see any of the snowy range from Skillet."

"Oh, Mama!" Becca pressed up against the wagon seat and pointed. "Look over there, at that beautiful house with all the trimmings. And it's got a tower on top."

Sure enough, the big house had a little tower on top, and around the gable was a wooden frill that Becca called trimmings. In front there was a porch with more trimmings.

"They must be awfully rich," Becca sighed. "I bet they've got a gold caster and everything."

"Well, anyway, they don't have a Star of Bethlehem like ours," Ernie answered. "Nobody has." That was what Papa would have said. He always set such store by that patch quilt.

They drove down the street. "Keep your eyes open for Parsons' General Store," Mama reminded them. "I hope we're not too early for Papa to be there."

They passed a livery stable and several stores and cabins before they saw Parsons'. Ernie drew up to a hitching post.

"You run in and see, Ernie," Mama said. "If Papa isn't there, find out the way to Charley Whiskers' ranch." She hesitated. Was that just one of Papa's jokes, to call him

Charley Whiskers? "I hope they'll know who you're talking about."

Ernie climbed down and went into the store. It was a large long room, dark after all the sunlight outdoors. There were counters and shelves and barrels full of all kinds of things—groceries and meats on one side, dress goods and boots and harnesses on the other, and all kinds of things in between!

A clerk was measuring out some dress goods for two women. He didn't even look up when Ernie came in. At the grocery counter two miners were getting an order filled. In the shadows at the back of the store, another man was opening some boxes.

Where was Papa?

Slowly Ernie walked over to the grocery counter. The man, who was measuring out some prunes, said: "Just a minute, son, and I'll tend to you."

"I don't want to buy anything," Ernie said. "I was just wondering if my father was here."

"Who's your father?"

"Mr. Willis Brett."

"Who?"

"Willis Brett."

"Don't recollect I ever heard of him. Is he a miner?"

"No, not anymore." Ernie's hands felt damp, the way they always did when he was excited. What if they couldn't find Papa? "He's . . . got a ranch now."

"That so? What's the name again?"

"Brett. Willis Brett."

The man shook his head. "Where's the ranch at, son?"

"Well, I don't know," Ernie answered. "We just came." Then he blurted out: "Do you know Charley Whiskers?"

"Charley Whiskers! Well, I guess I do. Nobody could miss knowing Charley—not with a face full of whiskers like that."

Ernie smiled. It was all right, then. "That's the ranch my father bought."

"Oh, sure. Now I remember a tall fellow in here the other day with Charley. Yep, that's right—Brett." He handed Ernie a few prunes. "My name's Parsons, son. You tell your folks they can get anything they need at Parsons' General Store."

"Yes, sir. Thanks."

"You'll probably find your Pa out at the ranch. Just turn to the right at the corner and keep going, past the

American House. You can't miss it. Charley's place is about three miles out, on the right. Big yellow pines by the cabin. Can't miss it."

"Thanks," Ernie said, and hurried out to the wagon.

The Surprises Come True

They had gone scarcely a mile past Nugget when Ernie, who was driving, suddenly shouted, "There's Papa!"

A tall man was striding toward them, walking on the high place in the middle of the road between the wagon ruts.

"Why, I believe you're right," Mama said. "I can't see his face, but he surely walks like Papa."

And Papa it was. Such a waving and shouting as they drew close together. Such noise and excitement when Ernie stopped the team. Papa climbed up to the seat, and Ernie jumped back with the girls. They all crowded close behind the seat so they wouldn't miss a word.

Papa had merry words for them all. "Did you get my letter about the surprises? Did you figure them out?"

He was bursting with plans. "Oh, there will be a lot of work for all of us, but looks like the best thing yet! Ernie and I will put in a patch of potatoes. Charley Whiskers thinks they'll grow all right, though the ranch is 8,500 feet above sea level. Then we'll have a crop of wild hay to cut in a few weeks. Ernie and I will build a root cellar, and maybe later, an addition to the house . . ."

Ernie and I. Ernie and I. That was what Papa kept saying. Ernie felt very proud.

"There's good water on the place," Papa went on, "and that's worth as much as a gold mine, you know." He looked at Mama. "I hope you're going to like it, Sarah. It won't be an easy life, and we'll probably never get rich, but . . ."

"I'm going to like being out of a mining camp, Willis."

Still, Ernie thought, she didn't actually say she was going to like Colorado Territory! She wouldn't go that far.

There was so much to talk about as they drove along. It seemed that Papa had been gone for a year, not just two weeks lacking a day. Then, suddenly, he drew back on the lines and called, "Whoa." When the wagon stopped, he listened and nodded, and seemed very pleased.

"Do you hear it, Sarah? The first surprise."

Ernie could not hear anything exciting. Only a kind of hoarse sound, coming over and over again. Becca wrinkled her nose. Florie stuck out her head and cocked it to one side.

Mama gave a quick start. "Frogs!" she exclaimed. "Why,

they sound just like the ones back home in spring. I haven't heard frogs since we came west . . . it's so much drier here."

"As if Michigan was right under your feet again, eh, Sarah?" Papa chuckled. "There's a little marsh on the ranch, you see. The land here isn't all rocks and mine dumps, the way it was at Skillet. You'll hear frogs croaking every spring."

"I'm glad," Mama said, as Old Nell and Jim started on again.

"I wonder if we'll see your surprise next," Becca said close to Ernie's ear. "Your watermelon."

"Watermelon nothing!" Ernie replied.

Papa gave his arm a big sweep to the right. The land rolled gently down to a broad green mountain meadow with patches of pines and willow brush at the edges. Rising back of the meadow were blue hills making curves against the sky, and off in the distance gleamed a jagged peak of the snowy range.

"Here's where our ranch begins," Papa said proudly. "It stretches half a mile along the road. As soon as we round the curve, you can see the cabin . . . and Queen Elizabeth."

"Who's Queen Elizabeth?" Becca begged.

"Why, Charley Whiskers says she's the queen of them all." Then Papa would say no more.

They rounded the curve. Down in the meadow, on a small rise toward the hillside, they saw the cabin. It looked very small and low, Ernie thought. On one side of the cabin was a log shed. On the other side were several tall yellow pines, one reaching high above the rest. Its trunk rose many, many feet before the branches began.

"I don't see any Queen Elizabeth," Becca pouted.

"You're looking right at her," Papa teased. Then he glanced down at Bibby. "If our Bibby grows up beautiful like that, she'll be the queen of Colorado Territory." He pointed at the tall yellow pine. "That big tree there is Queen Elizabeth, the queen of them all. When they logged this place a couple of years ago, Charley Whiskers wouldn't let them cut those pines."

So that was Queen Elizabeth! Tall and stately, just as Papa wrote.

They turned off the road on a faint wagon track leading to the meadow, and it was then that Ernie caught his breath. At the end of the meadow, with hills rising on both sides and another hill falling down at the back, he spied a little round lake. "Look!" he shouted. "A little lake. Is it on our ranch?"

"Yes, it's ours." Papa laughed. "Something round and cool, smaller than most, but quite big enough." Papa always enjoyed his surprises. "Of course, back in Michigan, they'd call it a pond. In Colorado Territory a pond makes a right good lake."

Ernie was excited. Only a small stream of water ran down Skillet Gulch. They had not lived anywhere near a lake since they came West. "I knew it wasn't a watermelon," Ernie said to Becca.

"The lake is fed by springs," Papa explained, as proud as if he had made it that way himself. "There is no real outlet, but some of the runoff makes the marsh for the frogs."

"The frogs, the tree, the lake . . . only two more surprises," Becca counted. She leaned close to the wagon seat. "When are we going to see the little cup?" She felt Florie pull at her dress. "And something the color of a thundercloud?"

"Wait till we get there," Papa answered. He pointed at the slope back of the cabin. "There's where we'll put the root cellar, Sarah. I found some fine stone back on the hill. It breaks off in slabs, and will be easy to lay up. We'll make a root cellar that will last a hundred years."

"Maybe we could have a stone house sometime, too," Mama said quietly.

"Why, of course we can. A stone house with an upstairs!" Papa's plans were always bigger and better.

The wagon creaked past the shed with its sod roof and drew up at the cabin. "Well, this is home," Papa shouted, and they all piled out of the wagon.

"Don't forget about the little brown cup," Becca urged, before anyone had time to look around.

Papa looked at her with a make-believe frown. "I don't see how we could forget about it, young lady. Not with you around. Well, come along over to the shed. The cup is in an old box Charley Whiskers nailed under the roof. I'll have to hold you up so you can see."

As they approached the box, just inside the door under the roof, something blue flew out.

"Oh, I know!" Ernie shouted. "It's a bluebird nest."

And so it was, the nest of a mountain bluebird.

"There goes the one on top," Papa explained. He boosted Becca up so she could look into the box. "Do you see the cup with the four inside?"

"I see four greenish-blue eggs in a cup of dry grass and bark. Oh, how pretty."

Everyone had to have a look. Then Papa turned to

Florie. "Only one surprise left. Aren't you going to ask what it is, Florie girl?" He waited hopefully.

Florie said nothing. She only looked up with shining eyes. Papa took her by the hand and led her into the cabin. In a moment she was out again, with a soft warm kitten in her arms. It was dark blue-gray, the color of a thundercloud.

"Charley Whiskers left it when he moved," Papa said.

"I'm glad the four-inside will be big enough to fly away before the soft-and-warm is big enough to find them," Becca broke in.

"So there we are—all the surprises." Papa started to unhitch the horses.

"It's a nice ranch, Willis." Mama looked around the hills, past the little lake, and across the meadow. "I believe we can make something of it."

"I'm sure we can." Papa gave old Nell a loving pat on the head. "The best is always ahead, Nell girl," he said. "But, of course, you know that already. You're a smart horse, at the head of your class."

Cornmeal and Dried Apples

The last potato was planted in the new patch. After supper, as Mama sat sewing at the kitchen window, she said: "We're almost out of flour and cornmeal, Willis, and I doubt if there's enough coffee left to grind for two more breakfasts. It would also be nice to have a few dried apples."

Mama kept right on working as she talked, so as to put off having to light the candle. She was sewing a buckskin jacket, trying to make the darning needle go in and out, but the needle always stuck. She had to push and pull.

Papa looked up from his old newspaper. It had cost twenty-five cents, and he was reading it for the tenth time. "Seems we'll have to be making a trip to Parsons' store. But . . . we're low on cash, and I don't like to ask Parsons for credit. Until the hay is ready to cut and we can sell some of it . . ."

Mama pushed and pulled at the needle. "I didn't want to say anything about getting so low on supplies while you and Ernie were so busy putting in the potatoes. Ouch! I guess a darning needle wasn't meant for sewing buckskin." She sucked the end of her pricked finger.

"You ought to have one of those three-sided needles for sewing buckskin, Sarah."

"I know, but I can get along without it for a while . . . until we sell the hay. One of those needles costs all of ten cents! Things are so dear out here."

"It's the freight," Papa explained, with a twinkle in his eye. "Hauling a heavy thing like that out across the plains!"

Mama smiled and got up to light the candle. Outside the light was fading. A soft blue haze from the mountains, like the dust on a plum skin, gently touched the meadow grass.

Papa put down the old paper. "I think we can start cutting the hay next week. As soon as it's dry, I'll sell a few tons to the livery stable in Nugget. Then I'll take the money and ride Jim down to Centerville and see if I can pick up some cows."

"I wish we had twenty pounds of butter to sell right now," Mama said. "We're that short of flour. How much do you think you'll have to pay for the cows, Willis?"

"It all depends. Some folks who dragged their cows across the plains may be glad to get rid of them at the foot of the mountains. Remember how old Kanter's cows got such sore feet he had to tie them up with strips of leather? I figure I ought to get three good milk cows for $200, say."

To Ernie who sat quietly whittling near the stove (so the chips would fall in the woodbox), that sounded like a lot of money.

Mama put down the buckskin, picked up some socks to darn, and turned to Ernie. "You'd better go tell the girls it's time to come in, Ernie. I believe they'd play under Queen Elizabeth till it was plumb dark, if I'd let them."

Ernie ran out.

"I don't like to say too much in front of the children," Mama said, after he had gone, "but we're short on everything, Willis. There is so much to do to build up the ranch, and no money coming in. Do you think we will make out all right?"

"Of course we'll make out. The best is always . . ." Papa caught himself. Ever since coming to Colorado Territory he had been saying that. Now here they were, starting all over again! Quickly he added, "Just wait till we cut the hay. I plan to sell about half of it now, and stack the other half. It will bring a higher price in winter. Hay is worth close to $50 a ton in Nugget right now, they say, and there ought to be eight tons of it in the meadow. Charley always was too busy looking for gold to cut the hay, but hay is the kind of gold I can understand."

Mama nodded. That was the way she felt, too.

Ernie came in with the girls, and Mama told Becca and Florie to get ready for bed. Ernie sat down at his whittling again, shifting his chair to get some of the candlelight.

Suddenly he asked a strange question. "Do people in Nugget camp like fish?"

"No doubt they do," Mama replied. "Why?"

"I was just wondering . . ." Ernie thought of the load of trout, in the bottom of a gunny sack, which Papa brought up from Greenhorn Creek whenever he had time to go fishing.

"Only," Mama went on, "I don't expect the menfolk in Nugget have much time to get out to the Creek to fish. Not when they work such long hours."

"Fish . . ." Papa looked up. "Ernie you're a smart boy!" He was full of sudden eagerness as he exclaimed, "Where's that old red shawl of yours, Sarah? If we're going to make some flies to go fishing with, we'll need a bit of color for them. Also, where's that old squirrel tail and those feathers? The fish will jump for flies faster than they will go for grasshoppers or worms. Why, I bet we can get at least fifty cents a pound for trout in Nugget camp."

"You mean you'll catch some trout to sell?" Mama asked.

"Sure thing. Ernie and I will be at Greenhorn Creek by sunup tomorrow morning. In a few hours we'll be back with all the trout we can carry up the hill. Then we'll drive to Nugget and sell them, and get that flour and cornmeal for you in time for dinner."

Ernie was excited. "We'll bring some dried apples, too, Mama, and . . ." He stopped. He had something else in mind, but he decided not to mention it. He would save it—for a surprise!

The House with the Tower

"I'll start with the boarding houses," Papa said, as he and Ernie drove into Nugget with more than fifty pounds of fresh, cleaned trout in the wagon box. The fish were packed carefully in damp canvas, under a layer of cool green grass.

"You pick out eight or ten of the nicest fish, and see if you can sell them at the big house." Papa pointed his whip at the white house with all the trimmings, the house with the tower. "You ought to get fifty cents apiece for them. Carry them in that piece of canvas, Ernie, and if you can't sell them there, try somewhere else."

"All right."

When Papa stopped the wagon in front of the miners' hotel, Ernie picked out ten fish that looked almost the same size. He hoped he would be able to sell them, first off, to the lady in the big house.

"If it comes to the worst, Ernie, we can always sell them to Parsons. Though, of course, we won't get as good a price from him." Papa started for the hotel with a bucket of fish. Ernie set off down the road toward the house with the tower.

It was a day of big white clouds floating like islands in a sea of blue. The sun swam in and out among the islands like a golden fish, Ernie thought. Only it was the kind of fish no one could ever catch!

The trout were heavy, but Ernie was too eager to care. He passed several houses and stores and, finally, the big house was right ahead. Anyone would have to strike a mine like the Crown o' Gold, he thought, to be able to own a house like that. In front there was a fancy iron fence, with a gate in the middle that had a row of little iron balls on top.

As Ernie walked up, a fat woman with hay-colored hair came around the corner of the house. She wore a red silk dress and looked younger than Mama, but not so neat. She carried a pail partly full of water. Then she saw Ernie.

"Hello," she said, in a jolly loud voice.

Ernie smiled timidly. "Are you the . . . are you the . . ." He didn't quite know how to say it.

"I'm Mrs. O'Malley, if that's who you're lookin' for. Wife of Patty O'Malley who owns the Lucky Strike mine." She smiled at Ernie. "My, you look the spittin' image of my brother Georgie when he was your age. You new here in Nugget?"

"Yes, ma'am."

"I'm just waterin' my posie bed." Mrs. O'Malley pointed to a few spindly flowers that were sticking out of the ground. "Patty—he doesn't want me to work, he only wants me to be a lady. Says I worked hard enough when I was young, waiting on tables and helping my Ma with the boarding house, but I fool him. I'm no hand to just sit around and be a lady."

"No, ma'am." Then, before Mrs. O'Malley could begin to talk again, Ernie blurted out: "Do you want to buy some trout?" He opened a corner of the canvas, and Mrs. O'Malley looked in over the fence.

"They're mighty pretty," she said. "Come on in, sonny." She opened the gate, and Ernie told her how he and Papa had caught the fish that very morning, and how Mama needed flour and cornmeal, and how they were going to get some cows.

"I remember times my Ma needed flour an' cornmeal," Mrs. O'Malley said. "She's well taken care of now, though, since I married Patty O'Malley. How many fish you got there?"

"Ten. They're close to a pound each. Fifty cents apiece."

"That'll be just right for dinner, if Patty brings some of the boys home, like he mostly does."

Ernie smiled to himself. That would mean he'd get $5

for the fish. With flour costing $20 for 100 pounds, as Papa said, $5 would buy . . . how much flour? Ernie couldn't figure it out, and, anyway, Mrs. O'Malley was talking again.

"The menfolk don't have time for fishing except sometimes Sundays. Catching fish on Sundays doesn't help much for eating on Fridays. Besides, Patty never seems to catch them a nice size like this."

"I picked these out special," Ernie explained.

"You don't say. Well, for that I'll give you an extra dime, just for yourself. To get some peppermint drops with, or something."

Mrs. O'Malley put down the water pail and took the fish. "You could count on my buying fish from you once a week, on Friday," she said, "and butter, too, when you get the cows. I'll be right glad to get some good fresh butter." She started up the steps. Then she turned back to Ernie.

"How would you like to see my new piano? Patty just got it for me last week. Had it sent up from Denver, and it cost $750. Only I can't play it."

Ernie had never seen a piano. Way back in his mind, he remembered the organ in the front room of the farmhouse in Michigan. Mama used to play it. But $750! How could anything cost $750? His eyes shone. It would be something to see that piano, and tell Mama and Becca about it. But then . . . he looked up at the house.

"Thank you," he said. "I'd like to see the piano, but I'd like to see the tower better."

Mrs. O'Malley burst out laughing. "Bless me if you aren't just like Georgie used to be. He'd have liked to see the tower better, too. Well, come along in, and I'll show you the both of them."

Ernie's Treat

Later, hurrying to Parsons' store to meet Papa, Ernie's head was so full of the things he had seen at the big house he could hardly keep them from running into each other.

The piano was big and shiny, but it didn't sound like much when Mrs. O'Malley pounded on it with one finger. The chairs and pictures and curtains and tables made Ernie feel dizzy—there were so many of them.

And the tower! The tower was wonderful. First you went up a broad stairway to the second story. Then you went in a little door, and up narrow, winding steps. Then you were in the tower, a room only as big as it was high, and all bright with windows. Ernie was sure he could see a hundred miles—the plains on one side, stretching straight into the sky; the mountains on the other, making zigzags against the blue.

"But," Ernie said to himself as he hurried along, "she doesn't have a Star of Bethlehem. I asked her. She said she'd give a lot to have a quilt like ours."

Old Nell and Jim were already hitched in front of

Parsons' Store when Ernie got there. He hoped he could buy the treat without Papa seeing him. Some peppermint drops, Mrs. O'Malley said. Well, lemon drops were good too, and licorice, but Ernie had another idea . . .

Papa was busy looking over some harnesses and talking to a man. Ernie went to the counter unnoticed, and put down his dime. He told the clerk what he wanted, and then hid it carefully in his pocket.

Sitting next to Papa in the wagon going home, Ernie was full of things to tell about. So was Papa! He was proud of the way he had sold the fish to the boarding houses without any trouble at all. "Why," he boasted, "they told me at the American House they'd like some trout every week."

"So would Mrs. O'Malley."

"That so?" Then Papa went on, full of eagerness. "I sounded them out about milk and butter while I was at it. They'd like to buy it from us."

"Mrs. O'Malley wants butter every week, too."

Papa looked down at Ernie, "Seems to me, son, you're turning into quite a salesman."

"She said I was like her brother," Ernie explained modestly. Then, in a flood of words, he told about everything—the red silk dress, and Mrs. O'Malley trying to be a lady, and the

$750 piano, and all the things in the parlor, and the tower . . . and, finally, the extra dime for a treat.

"What did you get with it?" Papa asked. "Peppermint drops?"

"No."

"Licorice?"

"No."

"Well, what?" Papa was eager to know.

"It's a surprise," Ernie said. He smiled, remembering how Papa always made them wait to find out about surprises.

"Come on, Ernie. Tell me." All the way home he kept guessing. "Is it gingersnaps? Is it soda crackers? Is it molasses candy?" But Ernie just laughed.

Only later did it come out about the surprise—after Papa had told all about everything at the dinner table, with Ernie getting in a few words now and then when Papa's mouth was full. "That Mrs. O'Malley gave Ernie an extra dime for a treat," Papa said.

"A treat!" shouted Becca, wishing she were a boy with fish to sell in Nugget camp. "What did you get, Ernie?"

"He says it's a surprise," Papa grunted, more curious than ever. "But I think it's time he told us, don't you?"

Slowly Ernie took a tiny parcel from his pocket. He handed it to Mama. "You open it," he said.

Mama undid the strip of paper, and there, at the end of the paper, threaded in and out, was a three-sided needle.

"Why, Ernie!" Mama looked at him in a special way. "That was real nice of you."

"Humpf," said Papa. "I had it in mind to get you one of those needles myself, Sarah, but Ernie beat me."

Ernie felt good. It was worth more than a whole sack of peppermints to beat Papa!

A Ride on Lake Michigan

Haying was slow, hard work. Papa cut it all by hand with the scythe, walking along swinging at the tall July grass. Ernie came after him with the pitchfork to shake the hay up so it would dry faster.

Later they had to shake the hay and turn it again, rake it into rows with a big wooden rake, and then stack it in cocks. Mama helped when she could; and Becca helped. Even Florie helped, by keeping the water jug full of cold spring water.

Before all the hay was piled in haycocks, it rained. That meant spreading out the last grass to dry all over again. Yes, haying was slow, hard work.

"We'll rest tomorrow," Papa said on Saturday night, after a week of swinging the scythe. "Even if it's good haying weather, we'll take Sunday off."

That sounded good to Ernie. He had not breathed a word of it to anyone, but his arms ached and his back ached and his legs ached. Sometimes he thought he just could not turn over another pitchfork full of hay, but he never let on.

Papa depended on him, and besides, he was getting a bulge of muscle that stuck out when he bent his arm.

Sunday morning, after a long night's sleep and a big breakfast, Ernie's aches were better. In fact, some of them were almost gone, but it was good to have a rest.

Ernie wandered down to the little lake and sat on the shore. Dreamily he looked across the blue-green water. It would be nice to have a boat, he thought, and go floating around. He wondered how deep the water was in the very middle. "Probably no more than five or six feet," Papa had said one time, but no one seemed to know.

"Ernie!" Becca called, running down to the lake so fast her sunbonnet fell back on her neck till only the strings held it on. "Come help, Ernie. Florie and I are fixing our playhouse, and Papa is going to let us use the cedar posts until he needs them for the corral. We have to have somebody strong, like you, to carry them."

Cedar posts. Ernie gave a start. Why hadn't he thought about those posts himself?

"Look, Becca, wouldn't you rather go for a ride on a raft than use the logs for a playhouse?"

"On a raft, Ernie! Oh, yes." She was full of plans immediately. "We could play house on the raft, couldn't we, and play traveling across the ocean . . ."

"Why not across Lake Michigan?" Ernie asked. "Mama says it looks like an ocean, and besides, we lived in Michigan once."

Ernie and Becca raced up to the shed where Papa was sharpening the scythe. They told him about the raft, for sailing across Lake Michigan. Florie flew in like a quiet little sparrow and listened.

"Well," Papa said, "I won't have time to build that corral till fall, and those posts will float like everything. I guess you children deserve a boat ride if you want one—the way you've been helping with the hay."

He put down the scythe. "I'll help you get the logs down to the lake, and we'll nail them together with some old planks on top." He picked up a can of rusty square nails that Charley Whiskers had left. "These will be just the thing."

Every log Papa carried down seemed to make him more and more pleased about the raft. By the time he was ready to nail the planks across, he thought it was all his own idea! Ernie looked at Becca and winked.

"There," Papa said proudly, as he hammered in the last nail. "That's a real raft, strong enough to hold an elephant. Ernie, you run to the shed and get that long aspen pole, and I'll give you both a ride across Lake Michigan."

The raft was wonderful. It rode high and dry across the little lake.

"Well," Papa said, when they got back to shore, "That was as good as a vacation." He handed Ernie the pole. "Think you're strong enough to pole it, son?"

"Sure I am." Ernie took the pole with a big smile, and pushed the raft along as if he had never, never ached from pitching hay.

Heap Red Strawberry Jam

The day finally came, after mid-July, when Papa was ready to ride Jim to Centerville to see about getting the cows. A nice stack of hay shone golden-yellow in the meadow. The rest of the hay had already been sold to the livery stable in Nugget camp. Papa had the money safely in his pocket.

"We did right well on the hay," he said, packing the saddle bags. "If I'm lucky, I'll bring back three cows, maybe four."

Papa was going to camp along the way. He took a roll of blankets and the old frying pan and a can to boil his coffee in. Mama packed as much food as she could into one of the bags, and put an extra pair of wool socks and a heavy shirt in the other.

"When do you think you'll be back, Willis?"

"I don't see how I can make it in less than five days," Papa answered. "More likely six. A lot will depend on the condition of the cows, and it may take me awhile before I can find some to buy. Better not count on seeing me before a week, Sarah, and then you won't be disappointed."

Somehow, Papa didn't seem as cheerful as usual. He went on packing in silence for a few minutes. Then he blurted out: "I'm a little worried about leaving you all alone out here on the ranch, with no neighbors closer than Nugget."

"There's no danger, is there?" Mama asked.

Ernie thought her voice sounded different. More quick. There was only one thing Mama was really afraid of, and that was Indians. She didn't even like to talk about them. Coming across the plains, she had always been afraid of an Indian attack. Afterward, in the mining camps, the only Indians had been friendly ones, but here on the ranch...

Papa seemed to read her mind. "I asked Charley Whiskers about Indians around here. He says they come through sometimes on their way across the mountains, but he never had any trouble with them."

Mama was silent. Carefully she skimmed the scum off the little batch of wild strawberry jam she was making from berries the children had found. "If only I knew something that would keep Indians away from the house!"

"There's the gun," Papa said. "You know how to shoot it. So does Ernie."

"That wouldn't do much good against a tribe of Indians." Mama dipped her spoon in the jam and held it up so the drops fell back into the pan. If they fell just right, very slow and thick, the jam was done. Drop, drop, drop went the bright red juice.

Just then Papa happened to look up. He gave a shout. "I have it!" He looked straight at the strawberry jam, and Ernie wondered what he saw in it.

"Sarah, you know that Indians run a mile from anyone they think is sick. Now, you just keep some of that bright red strawberry jam handy, and if you see any Indians, spot your faces with it. It will look like smallpox or something. The Indians will take one look and yell, 'Heap sick. White man heap sick.' Then they will disappear over the nearest hill before you can say Robinson Crusoe." Papa seemed very sure.

Ernie laughed, and Mama smiled as she said she hoped they wouldn't have to use the strawberry jam that way.

A Morning Caller

The third morning after Papa left for Centerville, Ernie was out digging a hole in the side of the hill for the root cellar. The ground was hard and dry, and the digging was slow, but he kept at it. He wanted to surprise Papa. In the thin clear sky, the big July sun stared down without blinking.

Ernie pushed back his hat and leaned on the shovel to rest. His eyes moved across the hill, past the lake, to the wagon road. There they suddenly stopped. Someone was coming along the road from the direction of Nugget camp. Ernie wondered who it could be. Few people passed the ranch, because the mines were mostly at Nugget or on the other side.

Ernie watched the man riding along slowly on a bay horse, leading a burro with a pack on its back. Someone going off to hunt for gold probably, but just then the horse turned to the right, down the track leading to the ranch. Who could be coming to see them?

"Someone's coming!" Ernie called as he hurried toward the cabin.

"Is it Indians?" Becca cried. She jumped up from the playhouse under Queen Elizabeth which Ernie had built for her and, dragging Florie after her, rushed to the cabin. "Where's the strawberry jam?"

Before Ernie could tell Mama about the stranger, Becca had her face all spotted with red!

Mama hurried to the window. "Thank goodness it's not an Indian. You never see an Indian with whiskers like that. It's probably just a prospector wanting to ask the way to somewhere. You run out and see what he wants, Ernie, while I tidy up a bit."

Ernie went toward the shed to meet the stranger. Never had he seen a man with such bushy whiskers. Somewhere under the straight nose there must be a mouth, but Ernie could not see it for the reddish-brown whiskers.

The man stopped his horse and looked down. "You must be Brett's boy," he said in a strangely gentle voice which came from somewhere behind the whiskers.

"Yes, I'm Ernie."

"Is your father roundabout?"

"No, sir. He's gone to Centerville to buy some cows. He won't be back till . . ." Ernie stopped. Maybe it wasn't a good idea to tell a stranger how long Papa would be away, but this man seemed nice and friendly. "He won't be back for a few days."

"Oh, I'm sorry about that," the man said in his low voice. He pulled his beard and shook his head. "I am sorry."

"Would it help any to talk to my mother? She's home."

The man swung down from his saddle. "It won't hurt any, I guess." He let the horse and burro graze. "It might do some good. How many cows is your father planning to get?"

"Three or four. With the hay money."

"I see," said the man, as they started toward the cabin. "By the way, perhaps you have heard your father speak of me. My name is Williams—Charles Williams. But, it seems, most people call me Charley Whiskers!"

Charley Whiskers! Ernie looked up in pleased surprise. "You are? Papa bought the ranch from you! Only I never thought you talked like that . . ."

"Like what?"

"I don't know—different."

Charley laughed softly. "I'm English. I've been over in the States eight years. I've taken out my first papers, proved up on a homestead, and grown a full set of whiskers. And you tell me I still talk different! That's what comes of being an Englishman, I guess."

They reached the cabin door. "Mama," Ernie called. "It's Mr.—"

Mama came to the door.

"Williams is the name, Mrs. Brett. But everyone calls me Whiskers—Charley Whiskers."

Mama was very pleased to meet Charley Whiskers. She shook hands and asked him to come in. Becca poked her head out from behind Mama's skirts.

"I say! Is the little girl all right?" Charley asked. "Do you want me to go for a doctor?"

Everyone laughed. Mama made Becca wash her face. Then they told Charley Whiskers all about Papa's idea for scaring the Indians.

Mama ended up by saying: "Won't you sit here at the table, Mr. Charley, and try some fresh-baked bread with some of that strawberry jam on it?"

"That sounds good to me," Charley replied, sitting down. "I don't often get to taste homemade bread. My biscuits usually turn out hard as rocks."

Mama brought him bread and jam, and poured coffee for him in Papa's big mustache cup.

"Well, he really has a mouth," Ernie said to himself, as he saw the whiskers open and a piece of bread go in.

Becca and Florie watched too, hardly taking their eyes off Charley's face.

"That was a meal I shall always remember, Mrs. Brett," Charley Whiskers said when he had finished almost a loaf of bread and a whole jar of jam. "Thank you kindly for it. Now I must tell you why I stopped by this morning."

It seemed like Charley had gone to Parsons' store early that morning for supplies for a prospecting trip. While he was there, a stranger came in to inquire about the nearest road over the Pass to the other side of the mountains. The man was upset to learn that the Pass was twenty-one miles away, and the road was none to good.

"Think I could get a cow over?" the man asked. "She's got bad feet and is due to have a calf in a few days."

"Do you have room in the wagon for the calf?"

"Nope," replied the stranger.

"I wouldn't try it, then," Mr. Parsons advised. "It's bad going."

The man grumbled. "I hate to stick around here waiting. I want to be on my way."

"Why don't you sell the cow?" Charley Whiskers asked. "I know someone who would probably be glad to pay you $50 and take her off your hands."

"She's worth more than that," the man said. "I brought her all the way across the prairies."

"I think $50 is about as high as Willis Brett would want to go," Charley said quietly. "He's just starting out on a ranch..."

After a great deal of talk, the stranger finally agreed to wait in Nugget until 3 o'clock. If Brett came with $50 by then, he could have the cow. Otherwise, the man would take her along and try to get her over the Pass, or leave her on the way.

"So, you see," Charley Whiskers ended, "there is a nice cow waiting in Nugget for you."

"Two cows," Ernie put in excitedly. "If she's going to have a calf."

"But," Mama sighed, shaking her head at Charley, "we don't have the $50. Mr. Brett took all the hay money with him to Centerville."

"I say, that is too bad." Charley pulled on his beard. "I feel a cow is a real bargain for $50."

"I'm sure it is," Mama sighed, "but I don't see what we can do."

"Mama!" Ernie's voice was eager. "We could sell some hay from the stack..."

"We couldn't do that by three o'clock, Ernie, and besides, Old Nell couldn't pull the load all by herself."

That was true. Papa had ridden Jim to Centerville.

Charley pulled a buckskin pouch out of his pocket. "I'd be pleased to lend you the money for the cow, Mrs. Brett. There is fifty or sixty dollars' worth of gold dust here. I won't need it. I have a month's supply of groceries on my burro."

Mama shook her head. "That's mighty nice of you, but we already owe you money on the ranch. I don't like to get too much in debt, since we're not sure how things are going to work out. Thank you, though."

Charley nodded and put back the pouch. "I understand."

Suddenly Ernie had another idea. He leaned over the table and turned the caster, remembering Mrs. Jenks. "We could sell the caster, Mama, and some other things to make $50."

Mama looked thoughtful. "We could. We could sell the caster, and the Star of Bethlehem quilt. The two of them together ought to be worth $50. But they won't be easy to part with, and your father will miss them. Still . . . Ernie, didn't you say Mrs. O'Malley had everything except a quilt like ours?"

"Yes, and she said she'd give a lot to have one."

"It would be a real nice home for the quilt," Mama said softly. She brought out the pink flannel bundle and undid it, so Charley Whiskers could see.

"I say! That's a real beauty, Mrs. Brett! If I had a place to put it, I'd buy it myself. The quilt alone is worth at least $50, without the caster."

"Do you think so?"

"No doubt of it. Mrs. O'Malley will be getting a good bargain."

Mama looked at the old clock on the shelf near the stove. "Ernie can ride Old Nell to Nugget and try to sell the quilt. He'll have plenty of time before three o'clock." She turned to Ernie. "Mind, now, you mustn't urge Mrs. O'Malley to buy it. You just tell her she can have it if it's worth $50 to her. I don't want her to be feeling sorry for us."

Ernie nodded. Then he listened carefully while Charley Whiskers told what the man looked like and what the cow looked like, and how Ernie should get a paper to show that he had bought the cow.

Charley rose to go. He thanked Mama again and wished Ernie good luck. "I'm heading south," he said, "where I saw some good-looking quartz rock last week." At the doorway he stood a moment looking out across the ranch. "This is a nice ranch, only I'm not a man who likes to be tied down."

"It is a nice ranch," Mama agreed.

Then Charley turned back and said: "I think the good Lord was feeling mighty happy the day he made this part of Colorado Territory."

The Deal's Off

"Well," Ernie thought, as he hurried along after selling the quilt to Mrs. O'Malley. "I didn't urge her. She wanted it right off. She even said $50 was too cheap for all those little stitches."

It was not yet three o'clock, but the man Charley Whiskers described was already sitting on the steps of Parsons' Store. He looked cross and tired.

Ernie hitched Old Nell to an empty post. He felt very grown-up, with a large-sized heart beating against his ribs.

"Are you the man with the cow that's going to have a calf?" he asked.

"Yep."

"I'll buy it. I've got the $50, and it's before three o'clock."

The man looked at Ernie and grunted. He rolled a wad of tobacco around in his cheek. "I'm not going to sell my cow to a youngster. How do I know you didn't steal the money? I can't trust a youngster."

Ernie stepped back as if the man had hit him. "I didn't steal the money. I sold Mama's quilt so we could buy the cow. Charley Whiskers said—"

"Said a feller named Willis Brett might want the cow. Are you him?"

"He's my father. Only he's gone to Centerville."

"Then the deal's off. Fifty dollars isn't enough, anyhow. Besides, I know the law isn't with me, dealing with a youngster."

Ernie looked at the man through a mist. "But . . . I sold Mama's quilt for the cow," he repeated.

"That's no concern of mine."

Ernie suddenly felt very small. He wanted to cry. What would Mama say if he came back home without the quilt and without the cow? What would Mrs. O'Malley think if he took back the money and asked for the quilt again?

Just then, through the mist, Ernie saw a bay horse coming down the street. It stopped in front of Parsons' and a man jumped off. "Hello, there," said a low voice. "Everything all right?"

Ernie ran his sleeve across his eyes, and looked up into Charley Whiskers' face. He felt like shouting, but instead, he said in a shaky voice: "He won't sell me the cow."

Charley looked the stranger up and down with his clear blue eyes, and spoke quietly. He said he would stand behind Ernie. "I guarantee you won't have any trouble. You just sign for the $50."

The man forgot all about raising the price. He signed the paper Charley wrote out and said, "Over there's your cow."

After the man was gone, Charley Whiskers told Ernie: "I was about a mile or so from the ranch when I got to thinking that a man might not be easy for a boy to deal with. I just had a hunch I ought to come back to Nugget to see that everything was all right. So I tied the burro to a tree, and turned around . . . and here I am."

Ernie looked up at the whiskers. He thought of a lot of things to say, but only two words came out. "Thank you," he said, but he said it for all he was worth.

A Strange New Voice

They were out looking at the cow the morning after Ernie brought her home. Ernie wanted to name her Mrs. Patch, because she had so many spots on her coat, like patches.

"I never heard of a cow named Mrs. Patch," Mama said, "but I suppose it's all right."

"Just so she isn't Mrs. Cross Patch," Becca broke in.

"She's not cross a bit," Ernie answered quickly. "She lets me scratch her nose and everything."

"I think we ought to keep her close to the house for a few days, Ernie," Mama said. "Otherwise she might roam off to have her calf, and we would have a hard time finding her. You stake her out to graze part of the day, and the rest of the time we can keep her in the shed, in the shade."

Ernie nodded.

That afternoon, when Ernie was digging away at the root cellar again, Becca sent Florie to the shed to get an old box for the playhouse. "It's right near the back, Florie, on the side where the door is," Becca said. "It's the box we stood on to see the bluebirds."

Florie ran to the shed. She took the rusty piece of chain off the bent nail and opened the door. Inside it was all dark, like the middle of the night. She stood at the door blinking a moment till she could see. There was the box, and there, not far away, lay Mrs. Patch. Florie started. What was that other thing? It had ears, and a nose, and a little white place on its forehead. Florie went close to touch it . . .

The first thing Ernie knew, Florie came running out of the shed, screaming. Behind her came Mrs. Patch. It was like a baby bluebird trying to run away from an eagle. "Mama! Mama!" cried a strange voice. "Becca!"

Ernie rushed with the shovel. "You stop that, Mrs. Patch," he shouted, waving the shovel in front of her.

At the same time, Mama came running from the cabin and Becca from the playhouse. Ernie saw that Mrs. Patch was excited and cross, but she stopped . . . and Florie was safe!

"Mama, Mama," sobbed Florie, as Mama took her in her arms.

Becca's mouth was so wide open that for a moment she couldn't say anything. Then she cried out: "Mama, she talked! Her tongue isn't hurt. Florie can talk!"

"Florie, Florie," Mama said, over and over again. It was hard to tell if she was laughing or crying.

Ernie was happy. There was nothing wrong with Florie! "Good for you, Florie," he said. Then with gentle words he drove Mrs. Patch back to the shed. When he reached the door, he understood why she had chased Florie. There stood the little wobbly calf, looking for its mother.

"No wonder Mrs. Patch ran after Florie," Mama said, when Ernie came back with the news. "She was afraid for her calf. Most cows are. She didn't know Florie wouldn't hurt a thing in the world." Mama looked down at Florie, who still clung to her skirts. "It's too bad you had to be scared like that, Florie, but you talked!"

"Mama," Ernie exclaimed, "what do you think? The new calf has a white mark on her head, like a star, and we got her for the Star of Bethlehem! Let's name her Star."

Long After Bedtime

"I don't think Papa will be coming any more tonight," Mama said the evening of the fifth day after he left. "We might as well go to bed."

It was not really dark, yet not daylight either—just sort of in between. In the west a few red feathers of sunset still glowed behind the hills, and the little lake seemed to be made of pink glass. Great blue shadows lay across the meadow, and dusky light came in the windows of the cabin.

"I won't even light the candle tonight." Mama put down the buckskin boots she was making for Bibby.

Just then, from the direction of the road, came a loud halloo. Everyone listened. Then came the shrill whinny of a horse.

"It's Papa!" Ernie exclaimed. "And listen to Jim calling to Old Nell." Then he begged the others: "Don't tell about Mrs. Patch and Star right away. Let's keep it for a surprise. Can I go meet him, Mama?"

"Yes, run along. I'll poke up the fire, and put on the coffee pot, and get out the bacon. Becca, you set a place at the table."

What a night of excitement. Instead of going to bed early, everyone (except Bibby—who slept through it all) stayed up until way after nine o'clock. All the things Papa had to tell! He was tired and sunburned, but full of good spirits and glad to be home.

"You ought to see the three fine cows I got, Sarah," he said, as he broke off a big piece of cornbread. "Ernie and I staked them in the meadow for the night." He reached for the last of the strawberry jam. "It's good to taste some real cooking again! Ernie, open that saddlebag. There are a few odds and ends in there you children might like."

Ernie opened the bag, with Becca pressing close to help. He undid a greasy piece of paper. "Cheese!" It had a hard yellow crust on it, but that did not matter.

"And sody crackers," Becca said, peering into a paper bag. The crackers were crushed and broken. Still, anything "boughten" tasted like a treat.

"Those gingersnaps at the bottom are for your mother." Papa said. But, of course, they all had some. It was a real party.

"Yes, I'm satisfied," Papa said, between bites of supper. "I got three good cows without spending quite all the hay money." He nodded his head and pushed out his lips, the way he always did when he was pleased with himself. "Now we've started a herd, all we have to do is build it up."

"I think four cows and a calf is a pretty good start." Ernie tried to make his voice sound natural, but he was pretty excited inside. He took the lantern down from the nail.

Papa looked at him, quickly frowning. "What's that about four cows and a calf, son? Don't talk nonsense. You helped me stake out the three cows yourself just now."

He pushed back his chair from the table, and reached out to pull Florie to him, setting her on his knee. "Well, anyway," he said, patting Florie's head, "here's one person who doesn't talk nonsense. Isn't that so, Florie?"

Florie looked at him with her big eyes. Then she said, "Papa," and buried her face in his coat.

At first Papa was too surprised to speak. Then he blurted out: "By Jove, Florie, you can talk! There's nothing wrong with you . . . you can talk!"

"It all goes together," Ernie explained.

"Yes, it all goes together," Mama repeated, as she lit the lantern.

"What does?" Papa asked. "Say! What's going on here, anyway?"

Mama picked up the lantern. "Follow us out to the shed, Willis, and you'll see."

"Well! . . . Well! . . . Well!" That seemed to be all Papa could say when he saw Mrs. Patch and little Star, and heard about Charley Whiskers' visit, and Ernie selling the quilt, and Florie being chased.

"Well! So that's what happens when I leave home. She looks like a good cow, and Florie can talk! But I don't like to think about that quilt. No siree, I don't."

"Mercy goodness," Mama said. "I think it's too late to be thinking about anything more tonight. It's long past bedtime."

"But I still don't like to think about the quilt," Papa said again, as they went back to the cabin.

A Surprise Trip to Town

The next few weeks went very fast. There was so much to do. Many a time Ernie wondered how they could possibly get everything done before cold weather came.

He was helping with the root cellar, and it was a big job. "No matter how long it takes, we're going to build a good cellar," Papa had said. "It will be nice and cool in summer and warm in winter. After we get through stoning the inside, we'll put on a strong pole roof and cover it with sod and dirt. Then in the front wall we'll fit two doors so there will be an air space in between."

Papa made a "stone boat" with logs for runners and a low box on top to hold stones. Then he hitched Jim to it. That way they could bring down stone slabs from the hill without having to carry them.

Then there were potatoes to hoe, and wood to chop, and fish to catch. They had milk and butter to sell, and a pole fence to build to keep the cows near home at night.

All day the cows were allowed to graze around the hills and up the meadow. Before supper it was Ernie's job to find them and bring them to the shed to be milked. He always rode Old Nell when he went for the cows. Sometimes they wandered so far away Ernie couldn't hear Mrs. Patch's cowbell. Then he would lean down and say in Old Nell's ear:

"Find the cows, Old Nell. You're a smart horse. Find the cows!" And the funny thing was, Old Nell usually knew just where to find them.

One morning after the cellar was finished and "most as good as a house," as Mama said, Papa suddenly remarked at the breakfast table, "Ernie and I are going to Nugget today. We're taking a ton or so of hay from the stack to sell."

Mama turned from the flapjack pan and stared at Papa. "You are! What for? I thought you were saving that hay for winter."

"I was, Sarah, but I changed my mind about it. I need some money."

"What for?" Mama pointed out that they had a good supply of groceries, what with the butter and fish money coming in each week, and their clothes would do for a while yet.

"I've got something on my mind," Papa said. "You might say the money is for a surprise."

There was no use trying to get a secret out of him before he wanted to tell. So Mama turned back to her flapjacks.

Papa never even told Ernie, all the time they were loading the hay on the rack and driving into town. As they jogged along the road, perched on the hay high in the air, they talked about everything except the surprise. Or else they just sat and bounced.

"The hills are mighty dry this summer," Papa said once. "I don't like that. Under the trees the pine needles are like tinder. If we don't get some good rains soon, the grass will dry up. Parsons said the other day it was the driest summer in seven years."

"Mrs. O'Malley is afraid their well will go dry."

"That's too bad. By the way, Ernie, I'd like to meet your friend Mrs. O'Malley . . . this very afternoon."

Coming home, without the hay but with a strange package in the wagon box under the hay rack, Papa felt very jolly, and Ernie knew why.

Papa began to sing at the top of his voice.

"That was a pretty good day's work," Papa said, when he finished the song. He slapped the reins on the horses' backs. "Your Mrs. O'Malley is an understanding woman, a mighty understanding woman. I'd have been glad to pay her more than fifty dollars. It's nice to have that extra money from the hay to our credit at Parsons.'"

"Mrs. O'Malley is real nice, isn't she?" Ernie felt like singing too.

"I wonder what your mother is going to say when she opens the package. Well, whatever she says, I'm glad to have the Star of Bethlehem back in the family again."

Smoke on the Wind

A few days after they brought the quilt back home, Ernie was helping Papa loosen the soil in the potato patch. It was a sultry August afternoon. The sky was full of strange clouds, pressing down, pressing down.

"Looks as if it's fixing for a storm," Papa said. "I'd begun to think the old sky had forgotten how to rain."

Ernie saw a quick flash of lightning cut the sky back of the cellar. He was not afraid. Still, the thunder was very loud and close.

A little breeze, heavy with the weight of purple air, began to blow. "Humpf," Papa said, shaking his head, "if we get a west wind, the storm might blow over before it rains at all, and we surely need the moisture."

Another jagged flash cut across the sky, seeming to split it open from top to bottom. Then a great crash echoed against the hills.

"I think we'd better get to the house, Ernie. It looks as if the sky could fall down any minute."

Hurrying, they left the potato patch and went toward the cabin. Just as they arrived, a third streak of lightning cut the sky, followed by the loudest crash of all.

"That was awfully close. I hope it didn't hit anything. I don't like dry lightning." Papa tried not to sound frightened, but Ernie remembered about the pine needles being dry as tinder under the trees.

Inside, the cabin was dark, as if it were evening and time to light the candle.

"I'm afraid that lightning struck somewhere near," Mama said. "Oh, why doesn't it rain?"

"I hope it didn't strike our playhouse," Becca said, running to the window.

Ernie went to the window. He saw Old Nell and Jim come racing down the hill to the shed. "They're scared," he thought. "I wonder where the cows are. Will they have sense enough to come home? Oh, why does the sky just hang there like that? Why won't it rain?"

Papa went to the door. "I'm going to take a look around. Just to be sure." He stopped in the doorway, sniffing. When he turned, Ernie thought his face looked pale under the sunburn. "I smell smoke on the wind! There's a fire somewhere! Ernie, come along . . ."

They rushed out. In the shed they grabbed two old gunny sacks and buckets. They soaked the sacks in the lake and filled the buckets. Papa said the wet sacks would be good to beat against the flames in the grass and pine needles.

"Look!" Papa pointed down the hill some distance below the lake, where a small cloud of smoke was rising. "The lightning struck all right, and the wind is driving the fire this way. If only we can get there in time . . ."

They ran forward toward the smoke, but it was too late. Already the fire had a good start. Its red tongue licked hungrily at the grass and dry needles, and leaped up to the lower branches of the pines. Smoke rolled up as the fire spread. Two gunny sacks and two buckets of water could not do much to stop it.

"Ernie," Papa shouted. "It's got too much of a start. And the wind is sending it right toward the ranch. Run back to the house and tell Mama to put as much stuff as she can in the cellar. Then tell her to get on the raft with the girls in the middle of the lake. Hurry . . . hurry!"

Ernie never ran so fast in his life. He could almost feel the hot breath of the fire on the back of his neck as he ran. Hurry . . . hurry.

Mama already knew! She and Becca were carrying things from the cabin to the root cellar, where they would be safe in the hillside, inside the stone walls. And Florie was carrying things, in her quick bird-like way.

"Papa said to get on the raft, in the lake," Ernie gasped. His heart was beating so hard he could scarcely hear himself talk.

Mama looked up over a pile of clothes and bedding. "Is it that bad, Ernie?"

"The wind's wrong. Papa can't hold the fire. It's coming up the hill. I've got to find the cows!" Ernie ran for the shed where Old Nell stood, her head up, her nostrils sniffing at the smoke.

"Oh, do be careful," Mama called after him. "If you don't find them right off, come back. Don't take any chances."

"We can't lose the cows, we can't lose the cows," Ernie kept saying over and over to himself. Quickly he put the bridle on Old Nell and jumped on her back. Papa said he had seen the cows on the south hill. Ernie turned Old Nell's head in that direction.

Old Nell sniffed and stomped. She refused to go south. Ernie tried to make her, but it was no use. "She's scared of the sound of the fire coming, and the smoke," Ernie thought. "I've got to find the cows and drive them to the lake!"

He let the lines fall loose on Old Nell's neck. "Find the

cows," he begged. "Find the cows." Old Nell raced off, east, down the meadow.

And find the cows she did! Not on the south hill, but at the end of the meadow, in the willow brush.

"Good Old Nell," Ernie said, as he hurried the cows back toward the lake. The smoke was billowing up now in big puffs. Wave after wave of hot air rolled up the slope toward the lake and meadow. The cows were frightened, but Ernie drove them ahead in the face of the smoke. When they neared the lake, they ran to it, wading out in the cold safe water.

Everything happened at once. Old Nell whinnied and Jim came racing down from the shed, splashing into the water. Papa came on a run, the fire almost at his heels, his face black with smoke and cinders. Mama and the girls were already on the raft, ready to shove off from shore, when Papa jumped aboard with Ernie after him.

Crack, crack, crack roared the fire as it leaped forward. There was no stopping it. Only the little lake was safe!

The Grass Will Grow Again

After the fire had passed, after that terrible half hour was over, the lake looked like an old silver dollar on folds of black cloth. Over the blackness hung a mist of smoke. The fire was hurrying up the meadow where the stubble was short and dry. The logs of the shed and cabin were still burning, the sides caved in, and, the rest of the haystack was gone, but Queen Elizabeth still stood, tall and stately. Her branches had been too high to catch on fire, and her bark too tough.

Now the fire was licking at the young pines at the end of the meadow, moving on in the direction of Nugget camp. If only it would rain! That was the one great hope of the little family huddled on the raft in the middle of the lake.

Then, down through the smoky, bitter air, a drop fell. It bounced on the water. Then another. And another . . .

"It's raining!" Ernie shouted.

Ping, ping, ping. Slowly at first, then faster and faster, the raindrops hit the lake and the raft. The burned shores of the lake began to sizzle and steam. It was raining! At last.

"If this keeps up, we can soon get to the cellar without burning our feet," Papa said. He sighed heavily. All his good nature seemed to be burned out, like the meadow, like the stretch of hillside below the lake.

"Oh, I'm so glad for the rain. Nugget camp will be safe now." Mama pulled her old wet shawl around her shoulders.

"And Mrs. O'Malley's piano," Ernie added. "Now it won't be burned up."

"They probably buried it in the yard when they saw the smoke," Papa said. He looked around, shaking his head. "Well, there's not much left. The potatoes will be a total loss. The hay is gone. And our house. And the shed." He gave the biggest, saddest sigh Ernie had ever heard.

"But aren't we all safe and sound?" Mama asked. "And isn't the cellar still there, with most of our things in it? And, look, Willis . . ." She pointed to a canvas bundle next to her and opened the flap just a little so the rain would not get in. There lay something wrapped in pink flannel, and, next to it, something made of silver and glass.

Papa almost smiled, but not quite. "The quilt and the caster!"

"Becca carried them down. I didn't want to trust them to the cellar," Mama said. "I was afraid that wet blanket I hung in front might go, and the doors might burn."

"Well, that's something, to have the quilt and the caster." Yet Papa was still sad. The rain splashed off his nose and got lost in his mustache.

Florie peeked out from under the wet blanket she had over her head. She held out a blue-gray bundle. "Kitty," she said, smiling.

"Florie means the kitten is safe, too," Becca explained. "That's something else."

"And what about the stock?" Ernie put in. "Mrs. Patch and Star and the three cows and Old Nell and Jim—they're all safe." Now that the fire had passed and the rain had come, Ernie felt very tired. He felt as if he could sleep and sleep, for a week, even with the rain pelting down.

Papa took off his hat and shook off the water. Then he put it on again. The brim bent down in a wave over both ears and looked very funny, but he did not feel funny.

"Sarah, my wife," he said sadly, "I've been telling you for four years that the best is always ahead, but I was wrong. I didn't get anywhere mining gold, and now the ranch . . . you can see for yourself. You didn't want to come west in the first place. Now I'm ready to give up. We can sell the cows and go back to Michigan."

Ernie shivered, as if the rain had chilled him through. Go back to Michigan! Leave the mountains and the little lake!

Sell Mrs. Patch and Star! Surely Papa knew that lightning would not strike like that again in a hundred years . . .

"Willis Brett," Mama exclaimed, after she looked him full in the face. "Do you really mean that about going back to Michigan?"

"Yes, I do. I know when I'm licked."

Mama's voice was strong. "Well, I don't. A year ago, two years ago, three years ago, I'd have gone back singing all the way, but not now. Something saved us just now—some power. We can't run away now."

Papa turned to her in surprise. "Are you saying you don't want to go back to Michigan, now you've got the chance?"

"That's what I'm saying, Willis. We had a dream in our minds of what this ranch could be. The fire hasn't spoiled our dream. The land is still here—it isn't even all burned over. We can live in the cellar till we build a new house—a bigger one, maybe even a stone one."

Papa stared silently across the water at the pile of smoking logs that had been the cabin.

"The grass will grow again," Mama went on, "now that the dry spell is broken. The meadow will be green again before summer is over."

Ernie watched Papa and saw him nod just a little.

"You said yourself you wished the shed was farther from

the house. Now you can build one where you want it." For once Mama was the one with the plans, with the hope, with the faith. Ernie was proud of her.

"And think, Willis, how lucky it was you sold that last hay. It would have burned up. Now we've got the Star of Bethlehem back, and some credit at Parsons.'" Mama's hair was wet, and partly coming down, but there was sun in her face.

"Humpf," Papa said. "Maybe things aren't as black as I thought." He wiped the rain off his mustache. "All of us together, maybe we can make a go of it yet."

They could, Ernie was sure they could, now that Mama wanted to stay.

"Of course we can," Mama looked off beyond the burned ground. At the end of the meadow the fire was steaming itself out in the rain. "I like this place," she said. "I like this whole country hereabout. Charley Whiskers said something that day he was over, I wish I could remember just how he put it . . ."

"I remember," Ernie said eagerly. "He said he thought the good Lord was feeling mighty happy the day he made this part of Colorado Territory."

THE END